# Three Little Pigs
## · THE PLAY ·

FEATURING:

## The Pig in Yellow

D1105153

### ALSO STARRING:

Pig in Blue
Pig in Red
Big Bad Wolf
Narrator

Adapted by Nora Gaydos
Illustrated by Barbara Vagnozzi

Narrator

Once upon a time, there were three little pigs. They lived in a hut with their mom and dad.

Pig in Yellow

**We are all big pigs now.**

Pig in Red

We have to go!

Pig in Blue

We will come back to see you soon, Mom and Dad.

**Narrator**

So the three little pigs said goodbye, and off they went.

**Pig in Blue**

We will look for a place to make our huts.

**Pig in Yellow**

**I will go up to the top of that hill.**

**Pig in Red**

I will go down by that white fence.

Pig in Blue

I will go under that big nest.

Pig in Red

Now what will we get to make our huts?

Pig in Yellow

**I will get grass and mud.**

Pig in Red

I will get sticks and twigs.

Pig in Blue

And I will get bricks.

Narrator

So the three little pigs worked all day long on their new huts.

Pig in Yellow

**I like my grass and mud hut.**

Pig in Red

I like my stick and twig hut.

Pig in Blue

And I like my brick hut.

Narrator

But a big, bad wolf was looking at them and licking his lips.

Wolf

Yum! The three pigs will make a good snack for me!

Narrator

So the wolf went to the hut of the pig in the yellow hat.

Wolf

(Knock, knock!) Little pig, little pig, let me come in.

Narrator

But the little pig saw the wolf.

Pig in Yellow

**No, no! Go away, wolf!**

Wolf

Little pig, little pig, let me in!

Pig in Yellow

**Not by the hair on my chinny chin chin!**

Wolf

Then I will huff and puff and blow your hut down!

Narrator

And he did! The little pig ran and ran.

Pig in Yellow

**I am too fast for that wolf!**

Narrator

The little pig ran to the hut of the pig in the red hat.

Wolf

(Knock, knock!) Little pigs, little pigs, let me come in!

Pig in Red

Oh, no! It is the big, bad wolf! I can see him.

Pig in Yellow

**Go away, wolf!**

Wolf

But I just want a little snack.

Pig in Red

No, no, no! Go away!

Wolf

Little pigs, little pigs,
let me in!

Pig in Red    Pig in Yellow

**Not by the hair on our chinny chin chins!**

Wolf

Then I will huff and puff and blow your hut down!

Narrator

And the hut fell down! The two little pigs ran and ran.

Pig in Yellow

**We are too fast for that wolf.**

Pig in Red

We will run to the hut of bricks.

Narrator

So the two pigs ran to the hut, and they went in.

Wolf

(Knock, knock!) I smell you, three little pigs.

Pig in Blue

Go away, you big, bad wolf. You will not get us!

Wolf

Little pigs, little pigs, let me come in!

Pig in Blue    Pig in Red    Pig in Yellow

**Not by the hair on our chinny chin chins!**

Wolf

Then I will huff and puff and blow your hut down!

Narrator

But the hut did not go down.

Pig in Blue

Ha! The wolf cannot get in!

**Pig in Yellow**

**Wow! I like this hut!**

**Pig in Red**

Me, too. The big, bad wolf cannot get us in here!

**Narrator**

But the wolf did not give up. He was getting very mad.

**Wolf**

This is it, little pigs. I will huff, puff, and blow your hut down!

But still the hut did not go down.

Pig in Blue

Look! We are still here. My hut of bricks is the best!

Wolf

You win, little pigs. I have to go back to my den for a nap.

Pig in Blue

We can all live here in my hut! Do you want to?

Pig in Red

Pig in Yellow

**Yes, we do! Yes, we do!**

Narrator

So the three little pigs lived together in the brick hut . . . and the big, bad wolf never came back again.